MY BEDTIME
Storybook

Illustrated by Peter Skinner

PRINTED IN GREAT BRITAIN
DEAN & **SON Ltd.**
52 54 Southwark St. LONDON SE1 1UA
TRADE MARK

The King's Cloak

THE King of Merryland was very excited. He had been asked to present the prizes at the Merryland Flower Show!

"My dear," he said to the Queen, "get out my best cloak. I can't afford a new suit, but my red velvet cloak will hide my old one very well."

The Queen ran up to the attic. She found the King's cloak in an old tin trunk. He had not worn it for a very long time.

The King hopped about excitedly. Then he heard the Queen squeal loudly.

"Oh!" she shrieked. "Just look at this!"

She shook out the cloak and this time it was the King who cried out. "MOTHS! Moths have eaten my lovely cloak. What shall I *do*?"

He hopped up and down in rage.

All over his fine cloak were holes, some small, some very big indeed. The King could not possibly wear it to the Merryland Flower Show!

He *was* upset! "I can't go to the Flower Show now," he said sadly.

"Don't be too sure. Maybe I can do something," said the Queen.

But the King went off to write a letter to say he could not present the prizes after all. Then, very unhappy indeed, he went to post the letter in Merryland.

He had to go through the wood first. As he went, the King thought of all the fun he could have had at the Flower Show. He was so busy thinking he did not look where he was going. There was a small stream in the wood.

Suddenly, plop! The King was in the water up to his middle.

The letter slipped out of his hand, and went floating away quite out of reach!

The King struggled out of the water. Ugh, how wet and horrid he felt.

"Why, Your Majesty," said a soft, friendly voice, "what have you done?" And there stood a rosy-cheeked little woman. When she saw the water trickling out of the King's shoes she said, "My cottage is near. I have a good fire, if it would please Your Majesty to step inside my humble dwelling."

"Th—thank y—you, m—my g—good woman. It will please m—me v—very much indeed," cried the King, whose teeth were chattering with cold.

The little woman led him to her cottage. Soon the cold, wet King was sitting in front of a fire,

with a nice hot drink to warm him up.

"This would not have happened if I had not been so upset about my fine, red velvet cloak," the King told the old woman.

"Tell me all about it, Your Majesty. Maybe I can help you," she said.

9

So the King told her how the moths had eaten the cloak he was to have worn at the Flower Show.

The little old woman began to chuckle.

"Hee! hee!" she said. "Here is a job after my own heart. Send me the cloak, Your Majesty, and I'll make it as good as new, or my name isn't Betty Thumbskill."

The King thanked Betty Thumbskill for her kindness, and hurried off to the Palace.

He was only just in time to save his fine cloak from going into the dustbin!

He took it back to Betty Thumbskill, but he did not see how she could ever make it as good as new.

"Call again in three days' time, and you shall see what you shall see," said Betty.

The next time the King saw his cloak he did get a surprise too! For clever Betty Thumbskill had taken her ragbag and over the holes those moths had made she had worked birds, fish, and brightly-coloured flowers. Some were of satin, some were of velvet, some shone like gold and silver!

The King *was* pleased!

10

He wore it to the Flower Show. Soon all the folk of Merryland were flocking to Betty Thumbskill's cottage to ask her to mend their worn-out clothes.

So, soon, although Betty's ragbag was empty, she was able to fill it with the money people had paid her to make their old clothes better than new!

Sam Squirrel's Lift

"TODAY," said Mrs Squirrel, "we are going to move into our new house."

"Good!" said Sam Squirrel. "What's it like?"

"Is it far away?" asked Sally Squirrel. "And why are we leaving Elm Tree Cottage?"

"Now that you two are growing so big we need a larger house," said Mrs Squirrel, "so we are going to Nuthole Villa, just along Hazel Bush Path."

"Will we have a bedroom each?" asked Sally.

"Has it got a nut storeroom?" cried Sam.

"Are there . . . ?"

"Wait now," interrupted Mrs Squirrel. "You'll find out all about it when we get there. But first of all you must help me move all the things. Now I'm going across to scrub Nuthole Villa, so that it's spick and span, and while I'm doing that I want you to take all the things from the shelves and cupboards and bring them across to our new home. Then when your father comes home he will only have the heavy furniture to move."

"All right, Mother," cried Sam and Sally, and as

soon as Mrs Squirrel had cleared away the break-
fast and set off with her scrubbing brush and pail,
they began.

"First of all," said Sally, "we'll carry down all the
vases, and then Father's books, and then the cups
and saucers from the dresser."

"We'll pack them in my wheelbarrow," said
Sam.

Up and down they toiled, from the little house in the top of the elm tree trunk to the ground and back again.

Soon their legs began to ache, and they sat down to rest.

"It's such a nuisance having to climb up every time," said Sam. "What we want is a lift."

"A lift?" exclaimed Sally. "What's that?"

"It's what people have to save walking up and down stairs," explained Sam. "Now if we had one we could just press a button and the things would be carried down by themselves."

He thought hard for some minutes, and then he cried, "I've got an idea! We'll *make* a lift!"

He scampered into the house and returned with Mrs Squirrel's clothesline.

"Look!" he cried. "I'll tie the things on one end of this rope and let them down to you, and then you can untie them and I'll pull the rope up again."

It worked splendidly, and soon all Mrs Squirrel's vases and pots and pans, and Mr Squirrel's grandfather clock were safe on the ground.

"Isn't it a lovely lift?" cried Sam. "We may as well let down the chairs now, and then Father won't have so much to carry."

"Oh, Sam!" said Sally. "I don't think you'd better. They're too heavy."

"Nonsense!" said Sam. "That's what lifts are for. Here comes Father's armchair!"

15

"Careful!" cried Sally. "Not too quickly!"

But it was too late. The weight of the armchair pulled little Sam with it, and, yelling with fright, he tumbled head first and hurtled towards the ground. But half-way down the rope got tangled up in the branches of the tree.

Poor Sam was left hanging in mid-air on one end, while Mr Squirrel's armchair dangled on the other end.

"Oh, Sam!" shouted Sally fearfully. "You'd better jump!"

"I can't!" sobbed Sam. "It's too far."

Just then Mrs Squirrel came back.

"Whatever are you doing with Father's armchair?" she scolded. And then, seeing Sam, she cried, "Goodness, my child, you'll be killed! Help! Help!"

At once all the neighbours came out to see what was the matter.

"Hold on tight!" "Call the police!" "Get a ladder!" Everyone shouted at once.

In the end Mrs Greytail got her thickest, strongest blanket, and all the squirrels held it out underneath the tree for Sam to drop into.

How glad he was to reach the ground again!

Then Fireman Nutkin climbed up his ladder and carried Mr Squirrel's armchair down on his shoulder. It was rather scratched, but Mrs Squirrel was so glad to have Sam safe again that she forgot all about being angry.

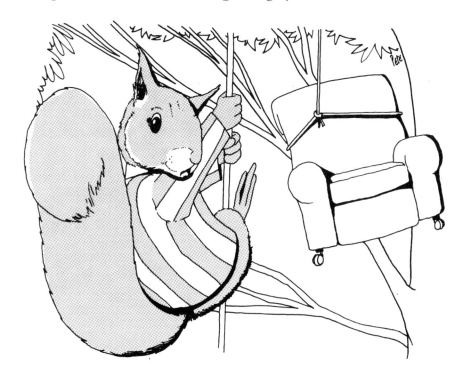

Pattikin's Picnic

IN the middle of Sleepydown Hollow lived the Pattikin Pixies, and the youngest of these, little Pattikin, had just had a birthday. All the other pixies had saved their money to buy him a tricycle, and it was a lovely tricycle. It was painted red and cream and it had a carrier on the back. Now Pattikin could do all his mummy's shopping for her. One day, however, he thought he would like to go on a picnic, all by himself.

Mrs Pattikin Pixie gave little Pattikin all the things he liked best to eat to take on his picnic. An egg sandwich, cheesecake, some coconut biscuits, an apple and a bar of chocolate. Pattikin put them in the carrier at the back of his tricycle.

Then off he went, along the road to the woods. On this road he met a dog.

"Hallo, Pattikin!" said the dog. "I am so hungry. Have you got something for me to eat?"

"I've got an egg sandwich, cheesecake, some coconut biscuits, an apple and a bar of chocolate," said Pattikin. The dog's mouth began to water.

"I do love chocolate!" he said.

So what could little Pattikin do but give his chocolate to the dog.

And then Pattikin met a fluffy kitten.

"Hallo, Pattikin!" she mewed. "I like your new tricycle. What have you got in the carrier?"

"I've got an egg sandwich, cheesecake, some coconut biscuits and an apple," answered Pattikin.

"Oo-er," purred the kitten happily. "I do love cheesecake," and she looked at Pattikin so pleadingly that he just had to give it to her.

Pattikin said goodbye and rode on. Presently he met a young donkey grazing in a field.

"Hallo, Pattikin!" said the donkey. "Come and talk to me because I am lonely. I am also hungry. Have you got anything to eat?"

"I've got an egg sandwich, some coconut biscuits and an apple," answered Pattikin with a little sigh.

"An apple!" brayed the donkey. "I love apples! Could you throw it over the fence to me?"

"I suppose I could," said Pattikin. He got off his tricycle and threw the apple to the donkey, who caught it between his strong teeth and munched it slowly.

It wasn't very far to the woods now. Pattikin rode on and came to a goat tied to a stake.

"Hallo, Pattikin! I was hoping you would come along. Have you anything to eat?"

"Everybody seems hungry today," said Pattikin, but he told the goat what he had left. An egg sandwich and some coconut biscuits.

"H'umph!" said the goat. "They both sound so nice I don't know which to choose. I think I'll have the egg sandwich if you can spare it."

Poor little Pattikin gave it to the goat, and it was gone in three gobbles.

"I hope I don't meet anybody else," thought Pattikin, but even as he thought that a flock of pigeons settled on the road near him.

They strutted towards the little pixie, fluffing out their tails and cooing. "Pattikin, Pattikin—have you anything to eat? We've come a long way, and we are all so hungry."

"I was going to have a picnic," he said. "My mother packed me an egg sandwich, cheesecake, some coconut biscuits, an apple and a bar of chocolate. I met a dog who ate the chocolate, a kitten who ate the cheesecake, a donkey who munched the apple and a goat who swallowed the egg sandwich. All I have left are some coconut biscuits, and as they are not much to picnic on, you may as well have them."

When he arrived home his mother had just finished making a cake.

"Why, Pattikin, you are back soon," she said. "I was just going to have tea. Have you eaten all that food I gave you?"

"No," answered Pattikin, and he told her what had happened to his egg sandwich, his cheesecake, his coconut biscuits, his bar of chocolate and his apple.

How his mother laughed.

"You had better not go on any more picnics by yourself," she said, "or you will be feeding all the animals in the woods. Now I'll tell you what we'll do. We'll take this cake into the garden and have our tea out there."

So, in a way, Pattikin had his picnic after all.

The Fairy Postman

THE sun was shining as the Fairy Postman made his way along the main road in Fairyville. His sack, slung across one shoulder, was filled with parcels and letters.

"Rat-a-tat-tat!" The Fairy Postman banged at the brass knocker of Fairy Snowdrop's cottage and slipped two letters through the letterbox.

Just as he was lifting the latch of another little gate, an elf, dressed all in brown, came running along the road.

"Have you a letter for me, please?" he called as he saw the Postman.

"Why, yes, Brown Elf," replied the Fairy Postman, and he searched amongst all the parcels and letters till he found a little pale blue envelope on which was written:

E. Brown, Esq.,
Cherryblossom House,
Fairyville.

"Here you are!" said the Postman, as he handed it to the elf.

"Thank you!" cried the elf. "It's from Fairy
Bluebell," he added as he read the letter, "and she
wants me to go to tea."

"Well, that's fine," laughed the Postman. "Good-
day to you, Brown Elf, I must be on my way," and
with a wave of his hand the Fairy Postman walked
up the garden path of Rosepetal Villa.

"Rat-a-tat-tat!" he knocked, and waited. Nobody came to open the door, so he knocked again.

A window above him opened.

"Who's there?" called the Wild Rose Fairy from her window. "Oh, it's the Postman," she cried, as she saw him standing below.

"Yes, ma'am," he replied, looking up at her with a smile. "And I have a parcel for you."

"Oh, how nice!" said the Wild Rose Fairy. "Now, I wonder, would you be good enough to open the door and put my parcel on the table for me, because I'm just bathing Baby Rosebud—and if I leave her for a moment she will eat the soap!"

"Certainly, ma'am," laughed the Postman, and after he had placed the parcel on the kitchen table he continued his journey.

Cottage after cottage he visited. Sometimes slipping envelopes through letterboxes and sometimes placing neat little parcels in eager hands.

His sack was getting lighter and lighter, and at last there was only one envelope left—tucked right away in a corner.

The Fairy Postman drew it out, wondering who

he had missed, for he had just called at the last
house in Fairyville.

"Good gracious!" he gasped. "It's for me!" And
so it was, for on the pale yellow envelope which he
held in his hand was written:

To the Fairy Postman.

Very Urgent.

"A letter for the Postman! How funny!" he said.

"You seem very happy," called the Woodland Pixie, as he passed on his way home.

"Yes. I deliver many, many leters, but, would you believe it, this is the first I've had for myself."

The Woodland Pixie strolled back and looked over the Postman's shoulder. "Why don't you open it?" he asked.

"Of course!" cried the Fairy Postman. "I do declare I'd forgotten all about opening it. I was so surprised!"

Hastily he slit open the envelope and drew out a sheet of creamy paper. There was a dainty golden crown on the top of the paper, and when he saw it the little fellow's hands shook so with excitement that the Woodland Pixie had to catch the letter as it fluttered out of his shaking fingers.

"Her Highness, Queen of the Fairies, invites the Postman to the Fairy Revels at Midnight," the Woodland Pixie read out aloud.

"Oh, how lovely for you," he cried, and shook the Fairy Postman by the hand before he rushed away, shouting his news down the village street.

Soon the Postman was surrounded by Fairies, Pixies and Elves, all trying to see the letter, and all saying how lucky he was.

As soon as he could get away, the Fairy Postman flew swiftly over the roof-tops of Fairyville, hurrying home so that he could dress in his smartest clothes in which to appear before Her Highness, Queen of the Fairies.

The Weeding Race

"SUPPOSE you have a race," said Mummy. "The two flowerbeds are exactly the same size, so if you weed one each that will be fair. And of course there'll be a prize for the one who finishes first."

Richard and Jane, who had looked unwilling when Mummy suggested weeding on a Saturday afternoon, thought this might be rather fun.

"I'll get my wheelbarrow to put the weeds in," cried Richard.

"What shall I have?" cried Jane.

"You shall have my shopping basket on wheels," said Mummy. "We'll put a large sheet of paper inside to keep it clean."

So they got everything ready, Mummy said "Go!" and they started to weed.

At first they kept stopping every minute to see how they were each getting on—but they soon found that if they did that they would never get on at all!

They didn't get on very quickly, anyway, for the beds were very large and covered with weeds.

30

Then the gate opened, and there was Ann with her puppy.

"Can you come out, Jane?" asked Ann. "Mummy wants me to give Puck a good run in the park because he's getting too fat. It would be such fun if you came too."

"Oh," cried Jane, "I wish I could. But Mummy wants the flowerbeds weeded."

"I'll help you," cried Ann, "then you'll be done more quickly."

"Oh, but that isn't fair," cried Richard. "It's two to one."

"Hullo!" cried a voice. And there was John with his kite. "Will you come and fly my kite, Richard? It's such a jolly windy day."

"Come and help me win the weeding race first, quick!" cried Richard.

"I've never done any weeding," said John, "but it looks easy." And he laid his kite down carefully in a corner and ran to help Richard.

"Mind the puppy!" cried Ann and Jane.

Puck had made a dive for the kite and was playing with its long paper tail! So after that he had to be tied to the lilac tree with his lead.

For the next few minutes it was very quiet, with the four children weeding busily. And then the gate clicked again and there were Grannie and Grandpa!

"Look, they're weeding—I love weeding!" cried Grannie, who was very tiny. And she began weeding with Ann and Jane.

"Come and help John and me, Grandpa!" cried Richard.

"I hate weeding!" said Grandpa, who was very tall. But he came and bent down stiffly and his long fingers worked very swiftly among the weeds!

After that they all got on beautifully.

"We're nearly done!" cried the boys.

"So are we!" cried the girls.

"Dear me—where have you all come from?" said Mummy, walking down the garden path with a packet of chocolate for the prize.

"We've won!" cried the girls and Grannie.

"So have we!" cried the boys and Grandpa.

"You've all won," said Mummy. "But the worst of it is, I've only got one prize."

And then there was the tooting of a horn, and it was Uncle Jim in his car.

"Good gracious, whatever's going on?" cried Uncle Jim, coming in at the gate.

They explained about the weeding race and Uncle Jim said, "I'll be the prize and take you all for a run in the country. You're mostly thin people, so I expect we can fit you in."

"The puppy's very fat!" cried the children.

Mummy hurried indoors to ring Ann's and John's home to ask if they could go, and the weeders got washed very quickly, and then they packed themselves into the car and away they went.

Uncle Jim found a hill which was just the place for flying a kite.

The puppy raced about so much everybody said it was bound to make him thinner.

Later they found a little café where the grown-ups had cups of tea and the children had buns and ices!

They all said they had enjoyed themselves tremendously, and that Uncle Jim was a splendid prize!

The White Fairy

THE fairies who lived in the little house at the top of the old oak tree all rushed to the window on Christmas morning. The snow was very deep and white, and each leaf on the oak tree held a little pad of snow.

"Isn't it pretty?" cried the Blue Fairy. "I'd like to have a day off today and have some fun."

"It's not your turn for a day off, Blue Fairy," cried the Green Fairy. "You had one last week!"

You see all the fairies had duties to perform every day; even on Christmas Day they were busy, helping boys and girls in all kinds of ways.

"It's my turn for a day off, I think," said the White Fairy, looking at the snow. "It's a white Christmas—please let me have today."

"Very well," said the Queen Fairy. "The White Fairy shall be free today. All the rest of you, off to your duties."

With a fluttering of many-coloured wings the fairies all flew off to their tasks, but the White Fairy glided gently to the foot of the tree and stood in the lovely crisp snow. She ran for a little way, laughing delightedly as her feet made tiny footprints in the snow.

"I hope I have an adventure," she thought. "I think I'll go down to the Big Lake and see if it is frozen!"

The White Fairy sang all the way as she tripped through the wood. It was so lovely to be free and not have to do any work. All that week she had

been working very hard, guiding little boys and girls home through the dusk and seeing that they didn't get lost or lose their school books and things like that. Of course, the boys and girls did not know that she was there, as she was always invisible to them.

Suddenly the White Fairy heard someone sobbing. As she came to the edge of the Big Lake she saw there were lots and lots of children skating on the ice, but right on the edge beside a willow tree sat a small girl.

"Come along, Joan," cried the others, but she shook her head.

"I wish I could skate," she sobbed. "I seem to fall over every time I try. It looks so easy, but I just feel too scared to do it."

Poor little girl. She looked so miserable, the White Fairy felt very sorry for her. Then she had an idea. Instead of remaining invisible, she made herself visible so that suddenly the little girl saw fluttering before her a fairy, as white as the snow on the ground. She was so tiny the little girl could hardly believe her eyes.

38

"Come along, Joan," laughed the White Fairy. "Follow me—little girl, follow me!"

Little Joan got up as if in a dream. She didn't want to lose sight of this wonderful fairy, so without knowing what she was doing, she began to skate across the ice, in order to keep the fairy in sight.

"Come along," sang the White Fairy, beckoning her on.

After her skimmed Joan, full of excitement, and when the other boys and girls saw her skating gracefully and rapidly across the lake, they did not know what to make of it.

"Look at Joan! Look at Joan!" they cried, following her.

Soon they were all skating in a long queue behind her. For a while the White Fairy flew here and there, around and about until little Joan began to realise that she was skating as well as any of the other children. It was all so wonderful she could hardly believe it.

"Oh, I'm so happy!" she cried. "It's quite easy now. A little White Fairy taught me how to skate!"

The other children looked around them, but they couldn't see the White Fairy, and when Joan went to point her out to them, she had gone! But Joan now knew how to skate and went proudly off across the ice to show them again.

When the White Fairy arrived home that afternoon, the other fairies clustered around her.

"Well, White Fairy," they asked, "how did you spend your free day? Was it fun?"

"Oh, yes!" cried the White Fairy, "it was wonderful fun. I saw a little girl in trouble and I—why—I——"

She paused in astonishment as she realised what she had been doing. "I've really been *working* on my free day after all!"

Then she laughed happily. "But never mind, it was every bit as nice as doing nothing!"

Tommy Turtle's Tricycle

"I want to buy a tricycle, please," said Tommy Turtle, scurrying into Mr Hippo's shop. "It's to be Grandad's present for my birthday."

"H'm!" Mr Hippo looked round his shop, then back at Tommy. "I haven't one in stock to fit your short legs, but I can get one specially for you."

"How soon?" asked Tommy.

"Oh, by tomorrow. Call in on your way from school."

"I'm not going to tell the others or they'll all want to ride it, and perhaps break it," Tommy said to himself next afternoon. Full of excitement, he slipped away to Mr Hippo's shop again while his friends were playing.

"Well, how will *that* do?" Mr Hippo asked him.

Tommy pedalled the tricycle up and down the shop, then said it would do nicely, and off he went to try riding it home along the sand.

"If I cycle near the sea, the rocks will hide me from the others if they come along," he said to himself.

His short little legs worked hard sending the tricycle out quite a long way, leaving deep tracks behind it. But the closer he got to the sea, the softer the sand was of course, and soon the tricycle was simply ploughing a way through it instead of bowling over it.

The other turtle-boys soon missed Tommy, so they went to look for him, thinking perhaps he had slipped away to call at Mrs Brownbear's shop for honeydrops on his way home. But as they passed Mr Hippo's shop he called out in a friendly way, and in the hope of more orders:

"What do you think of Tommy's tricycle, boys?"

"Tricycle?" they echoed, in great surprise.

"Yes, his new one. He has gone home on it."

Off they dashed at this news, the marks on the sand soon telling them which way to go.

"Ha!" cried one turtle-boy. "We're on the right track, though we shouldn't have known what the marks meant if Mr Hippo hadn't spoken."

Just at that moment they heard a yell.

"Come on!" cried the leader. "Perhaps old Tommy has hurt himself."

But all that was to be seen when they reached Tommy was his head above the soft sand.

"Help!" he cried on seeing his friends. "My tricycle has sunk, and I can't get it up."

By holding on to each other in a kind of chain, the turtle-boys at last hauled Tommy and his tricycle out of the soft sand, and Tommy looked at them gratefully when his treasure was safe.

"It was silly of me to get so near the water," he said, ashamed to tell them why he had done it. "Come along, all of you, and we'll take turns riding home."

Tommy felt all the happier for sharing his tricycle, and now all the turtle-boys have tricycles of their own, for Mr Hippo got quite a lot of orders as birthdays came round!